Eric Veillé

Encyclopedia of Grannies

Translated by Daniel Hahn

GECKO PRESS

This edition first published in 2019 by Gecko Press
PO Box 9335, Wellington 6141, New Zealand
info@geckopress.com

English-language edition © Gecko Press Ltd 2019
Translation © Daniel Hahn 2019
L'encyclopédie des mamies © Actes Sud, France 2018

Illustrations created in brush pens on paper then
reworked digitally and printed in four spot inks.

Edited by Penelope Todd
Typeset in Gotham by Katrina Duncan
Printed in China by Everbest Printing Co. Ltd,
an accredited ISO 14001 & FSC certified printer

ISBN: 978-1-776572-43-4

For more curiously good books, visit geckopress.com

Grannies

There are so many grannies...

Young
grannies...

grannies in
ski suits...

Australian
grannies.

Grannies from
the salt flats...

city grannies...

and country
grannies.

Grannies who
love nature...

and grannies of
the South Seas.

Inside

Have you seen inside a granny?

Inside every granny, there's a small house, and in that house is that same granny when she was a little girl. That's where she still lives.

Oh, YEah.

CuTE!

Nicknames

Every granny has a nickname.
For example:

Nana

Gran

Oma

Mimi

Meemaw

Abuela

Nani

Gigi

Nonna

Bubbe

G-ma

Time

Grannies are the only people who always have time...

Time to laugh with their friends.

Time to straighten a bra strap.

Time to get names muddled.

Time to be tempted by a cream bun.

HOW'S MICHELLE? Er...DaniELLE?

Time to give us cuddles.

Time to open oysters.

TIME TO LEARN hOW TO LiVE. NOPE—TOO LaTE FOR ThaT NOW.

Time to give the table a quick wipe.

Wisdom

Grannies know a lot of things!
So let's make sure to ask them
the important questions:

Sayings

To really understand grannies,
there's nothing like a good saying:

When grannies take showers,
you'll be waiting for hours.

Grans behind shutters
are probably nutters.

Grans in the rain
seldom complain.

Grannies at the store
can never find the door.

Grans will go far
to teach you to spar.
(Whoever you are.)

Once Granny's
dressed for bed
there's no more
to be said.

Granny likes a peaceful house.
Quiet as a mouse!

Grannies need thrones
to rest their old bones.

Flexibility

Please admire how very flexible grannies can be.

Splits

Legs up

Handstand

Big leap
with shower
curtain

Double tuck

Oops.
Gently does it.

Squat

Run-up

Take-off

Rest

Hiding places

It's amazing how many hiding places you can find in a granny's house when you think about it.

The waiting room

When you arrive in a waiting room,
there's always a granny already there.

Grannies' moods

Sometimes a granny feels like a lump of old mashed potato, which is a sign that she's not doing great.

It's pretty unusual, and not many people know this, but grannies can sometimes be sad, or in a bad mood.

MaYBE THEY'RE FED uP WiTH BEiNG OLD.

If you want to raise a granny's spirits, you can:

Draw her a chicken.

Ta-Da!

Put her hair in pigtails.

DonE!

Peel her an orange.

nEarLY THErE

Tell her a secret.

"You KnOW, i DOn't actuaLLY LiKE SPinach."

"Oh, rEaLLY?"

Play her a bit of Rachmaninov.

...ThrEE, Four...

Take her to Lapland.

"TErVETuLOa"

Give her drops of rain from countries where it doesn't rain.

"Thanks, you ShouLDn't haVE."

Scratch her back.

ScraTch, ScraTch

Teach her Spanish.

"POLLO Y PaTaTas?"

"EXCELLEnT."

Granny borealis

If you want to see a granny borealis,
you need to stay up late
and trust in fate.

Inside granny's bed

It's not often you have the chance to slip into a granny's bed. However, if you do, have a good rummage and you might find:

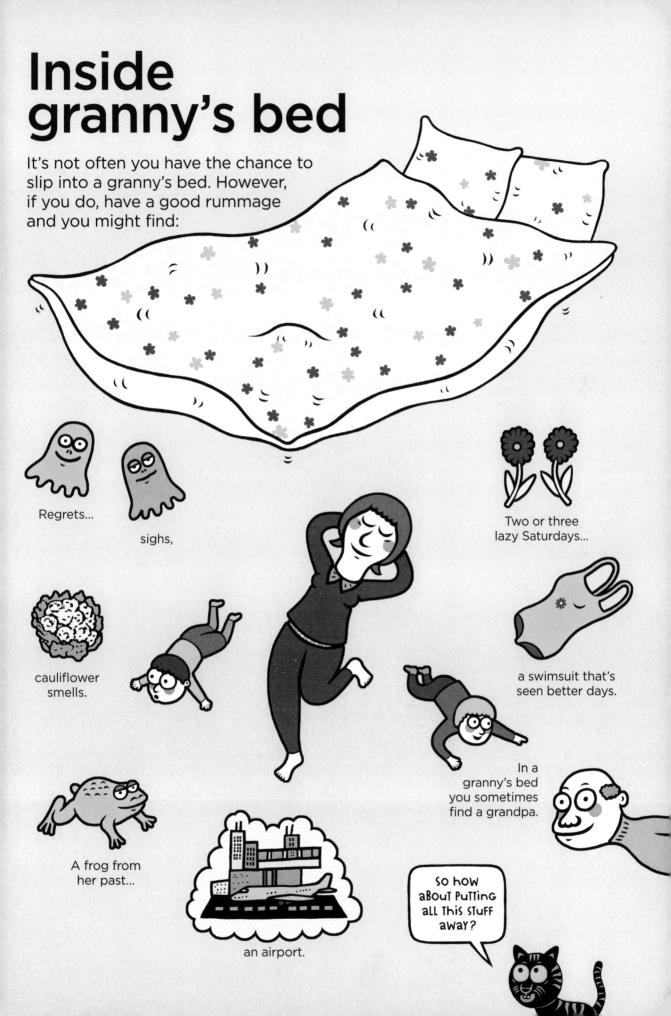

Regrets...

sighs,

cauliflower smells.

Two or three lazy Saturdays...

a swimsuit that's seen better days.

A frog from her past...

In a granny's bed you sometimes find a grandpa.

an airport.

SO HOW aBOUT PUTTING ALL THIS STUFF away?

Hair

Most grannies do whatever they like
with their hair. And quite right.

"The Fan"

"The Tea Cosy"

"The Waterfall"

"The Scramble"

"The Wave"

"The Coral"

"The Tower"

"The Crop"

OK, this one's just weird.

Forest grannies

Rain or shine, these grannies are crazy about taking walks in nature.

Buses

Why do grannies travel on buses?

It's true that you
often see grannies
behind bus windows.

But nobody knows
where they go.

GOOD QUESTION.

All we know is
that they prefer
the seat nearest
the driver, so there's
room for their legs.

228·PKQ·2

DON'T STICK
THEM OUT
TOO FAR.

Cats

A few grannies can understand cat language.
The rest don't get it at all.

Postcards

If you send your granny a card
you'll make her day—it's not hard.

VITRAC

МосквА

Dear Gran,
I think about
you whenever
I have time.
Love, Mimi

Happy Sunday

hUGS FROM TaraPoTo

Grandma, I got
sand in my
eyes and my
brother failed
chemistry. Sending
you a kiss
—Louis

Greetings from ROCHDALE

LE MANS

Dear Nana,
I'm in Germany
but I can't
really tell
the difference.
But I got my
cast off!
Yasmina

GRÖMITZ

GRANNIE'S MAIL

Darling Granny,
If you're sick of
doing the laundry
it's okay to tell me.
Marie-Pierre
Planchon

Grannies and their travels

When they get bored, some grannies pull on a pair of slippers and head off around the world.

Burkina Faso in slippers.

Senegal in slippers.

The Andes in slippers.

Martinique in slippers...

...even Machu Picchu in slippers!

When they get hungry, a pastry slips down nicely.

And when it's time to rest, they slip on some Grans N' Roses...

(When granddads go with them, they wear flippers.)

Vocabulary

These are the words you need to know if you want a better understanding of grannies:

Away
A place where lots of grannies go. They'll say, for example, "The week of August 15th, I'll be away."

Creepy-crawlies
Insects you can annoy when you get bored at Granny's.

Hair back
When Granny's hair is combed back, there's a storm brewing. Best to stay under cover.

Discount coupons
Grannies have discount coupons, which they use to buy vegetables for themselves, or toys for us.

Night cream
Grannies go crazy with their night cream. They put it on after the eight o'clock news and, if all goes well, they'll look radiant in the morning.

Boat
I know it's incredible, but some grannies have no idea how to draw a boat.

Family trees
These trees are full of people you don't know.

"WOULD YOU LIKE TO DANCE, GRANDMA?"

"HUSH, NOW."

Uncle
At weddings, grannies sometimes dance with uncles.

Forgetting
It can happen that grannies forget to buy toilet paper. Still, it's no big deal.

Reading list

There are a few books about grannies
that aren't too bad: